Yo Ho Ho,
A Pirate's Christmas!

Book by James J. Mellon

Music and Lyrics by
Scott DeTurk and James J. Mellon

A SAMUEL FRENCH ACTING EDITION

SAMUEL FRENCH

FOUNDED 1830

SAMUELFRENCH.COM

No one shall commit or authorize any act or omission by which the copyright of, or the right to copyright, this play may be impaired.

No one shall make any changes in this play for the purpose of production.

Publication of this play does not imply availability for performance. Both amateurs and professionals considering a production are strongly advised in their own interests to apply to Samuel French, Inc., for written permission before starting rehearsals, advertising, or booking a theatre.

No part of this book may be reproduced, stored in a retrieval system, or transmitted in any form, by any means, now known or yet to be invented, including mechanical, electronic, photocopying, recording, videotaping, or otherwise, without the prior written permission of the publisher.

RENTAL MATERIALS

An orchestration consisting of **Piano/Conducter's Score and Accompaniment CD** will be loaned two months prior to the production ONLY on the receipt of the Licensing Fee quoted for all performances, the rental fee and a refundable deposit.

Please contact Samuel French for perusal of the music materials as well as a performance license application.

IMPORTANT BILLING AND CREDIT
REQUIREMENTS

All producers of *YO HO HO, A PIRATE'S CHRISTMAS!* *must* give credit to the Authors of the Play in all programs distributed in connection with performances of the Play, and in all instances in which the title of the Play appears for the purposes of advertising, publicizing or otherwise exploiting the Play and/or a production. The name of the Authors *must* appear on a separate line on which no other name appears, immediately following the title and *must* appear in size of type not less than fifty percent of the size of the title type.

YO HO HO, A PIRATE'S CHRISTMAS! was first produced by Open at the Top Productions in The Noho Arts Center from November 30 to December 30, 2007. The performance was directed by James J. Mellon, with sets by Craig Siebels, costumes by Shon LeBlanc, and lighting by Luke Moyer. The cast was as follows:

BLACK EYED JOHNNY . . . . Jonathan Zenz

GRAINNE O'MALLY . . . . Melanie Ewbank

RUBY RED. . . . . .Holly Persel

BILLY GOAT . . . . Billie Puyear

WINKY. . . . . .Alex Holmes

TUSK. . . . . JR Mangels

JUNKMAN JAKE . . . . Bonnie Cahoon

JIMMY JACK . . . . .Will Rose-Hines, Matthew Shane

EVE CHRISTMAS. . . . . Daisy Bishop, Nora James Rose-Hines,
Danielle Soibelman

MURRAY CHRISTMAS . . . . Brian Coffee

HAPPY CHRISTMAS . . . . Janet Fontaine

HOLLY CHRISTMAS. . . . . .Allie Costa

IVY CHRISTMAS . . . . Kennedy Heidel

MRS. CLAUS . . . . .Jo Jordon

SANTA CLAUS. . . . . Michael Catlin

CHARACTERS

BLACK EYED JOHNNY

GRAINNE O'MALLY

RUBY RED

WINKY

TUSK

JUNKMAN JAKE

JIMMY JACK

EVE CHRISTMAS

MURRAY CHRISTMAS

HAPPY CHRISTMAS

HOLLY CHRISTMAS

IVY CHRISTMAS

MRS. CLAUS

SANTA CLAUS

MUSICAL NUMBERS

I Wouldn't Mind . . . . **EVE**

Sail On. . . . . **THE PIRATES**

Snow . . . . **THE PIRATES**

Where are They Now . . . . **EVE, HAPPY, HOLLY, IVY, MURRAY**

Petey's Song. . . . . **EVE, PETEY, TUSK, WINKY**

Yo Ho Ho/Ho Ho Ho . . . . **THE PIRATES AND THE ELVES**

If Women Ruled the World. . . . . **EVE, GRAINNE O'MALLY, HAPPY,**
MRS. SANTA, THE WOMEN

Christmas Is All About The Love . . . . **ALL**

Sail On Finale . . . . **ALL**

*(Music: #1 **SHOW OPENING**)*

(From the darkness we hear a soft melody, a Pirate's tune, but beautifully played. An ominous sound creeps into the music, finishing with a rousing cannon fire.)

(A pool of light shines on a young girl jumping on her bed. She is dressed for sleep and it is clearly Christmas Eve. She is playing Pirate Ship and has a wrapping paper roll as her sword.)

EVE. Ahoy! Don't you be tryin' to run away from me. I'll not be hornswaggled, I won't. I'm as strong as any Pirate Lad there ever was.

(making the sound of cannons blazing with her mouth)

(From offstage we hear a voice:)

HAPPY. Eve, it's time for bed. Settle down in there!

EVE. *(turning to the voice)* You ought not to talk to me like that. Not to Black Eyed Johnny!

IVY. *(coming to the banister)* Mom! Tell her to shut up, I can't hear myself think.

EVE. *(to **IVY**)* Put one hoof on this barge and you'll wish you hadn't.

HOLLY. You keep screaming like that and you'll wish a lot of things.

*(**MURRAY** enters and looks up to **HOLLY** and **IVY**.)*

MURRAY. Alright you two, go say good-night to your aunt and uncle and then get back to bed. I'll handle your sister.

*(to **EVE** from outside of her room)*

Ahoy, Captain, askin' permission to come aboard!

EVE. We're takin' no weight, we're not! I'm the captain of this here vessel, and if you try to board her, I'll have ye' swimmin' with the sharks...

(**MURRAY**'s *brother,* **KRIS,** *comes up behind him and laughs. He rushes in and pretends to be one of her pirates.*)

KRIS. Captain, they're comin' from everywhere. What're we gonna do? Should we man the cannons?

EVE. *(surprised by Kris, dropping character for a moment)* Do we have cannons?

MURRAY. *(playing along)* Ahah! Caught off guard. This whole vessel is surrounded by reindeer. There's no escape.

(**MURRAY, KRIS,** *and* **EVE** *begin to battle as* **HAPPY** *enters with her sister,* **NOEL.** *She carries* **EVE**'s *doll and starts tucking her into bed.*)

HAPPY. Alright, alright. Thanks for the help Murray. You were supposed to be quieting her down.

EVE. *(posing on the bedpost)* There's no quieting Black Eyed Johnny. His voice is to be heard from far and wide!

NOEL. Oh, sweetie, I think Santa might be too frightened to stop by your house with so much treachery going on.

EVE. I don't think so.

KRIS. Santa's not afraid of anything.

NOEL. *(to* **KRIS***)* Thanks, Kris. Good to know.

HAPPY. Well, it's time to put away the sword and tuck yourself into your bed. Say good night to aunt Noel and uncle Kris.

(**EVE** *runs into* **KRIS**'s *arms and gets a hug. She hugs* **NOEL** *and gets into bed.*)

KRIS. *(leaning in to Eve)* You just don't worry. Santa will be here tonight. You can count on it.

EVE. I know.

HAPPY. I brought your doll up from the living room.

(**EVE** *crawls into bed and takes her doll with her.*)

EVE. Mom, do you think if I wanted to I could grow up and become a pirate?

NOEL. Honey, why would you want to be a pirate? Why not a princess?

KRIS. Pirates are more fun.

HAPPY. Good to know Kris, thank you.

NOEL. He's just a font of information. Really.

(**HAPPY** *motions for* **MURRAY** *to say something.*)

MURRAY. Sweetie, you can be anything you want to be. The problem is, there's really no such thing as pirates any more. They're only in the movies.

EVE. *(grabbing her sword back from her mother)* Arrgh! You shouldn't be sayin' that to Black Eyed Johnny, mate. I'll have ye walkin' the plank for sayin' somethin' like that...

HAPPY. Alright, alright. Let's not any of us be walking any plank on Christmas Eve. Why don't you go to sleep and dream of sugar plum fairies dancing in your head.

EVE. *(charmingly sarcastic)* Mom, have you ever actually seen a sugar plum fairy?

HAPPY. As a matter of fact...

EVE. Mom...for real.

HAPPY. *(backtracking)* Well, I mean...

EVE. Exactly!

(**KRIS** *starts to laugh.* **NOEL** *and* **HAPPY** *look at him.* **MURRAY** *is stifling a laugh as well.*)

(*From above,* **HOLLY** *and* **IVY** *peer over the banister.*)

IVY. I thought we were supposed to be asleep by now.

HOLLY. Yeah, that's what you told us.

MURRAY. *(to* **HOLLY** *&* **IVY***)* Go back to bed. We'll be in to say good-night in a minute.

NOEL. We'll go say good-night to the girls. *(to* **KRIS***)* Let's go Captain Hook.

KRIS. *(as he exits)* Ho Ho Ho!

(**NOEL** *and* **KRIS** *exit.*)

(**EVE** *crawls into bed and is tucked in.*)

MURRAY. Good night, my beautiful pirate queen. Happy dreams.

HAPPY. See you in the morning, sweetie.

EVE. Did you put out the carrots for the reindeers?

HAPPY. Of course. Now go to sleep.

EVE. What about the cookies?

MURRAY. They're out.

EVE. And the milk?

HAPPY. Everything Santa could ever want is on our kitchen table and if he doesn't find what he's looking for he can always look in the refrigerator. Now go to sleep.

(Music: #2 **I WOULDN'T MIND***)*

*(***HAPPY** *and* **MURRAY** *begin to exit.* **MURRAY** *turns out the lights and the two of them look on as* **EVE** *starts to drift off to sleep. They exit.)*

*(***EVE** *bolts up in bed, looking towards the sky.)*

EVE. *(whispering)* Alright, I think we should have just one more conversation before I go to sleep. Just to make sure. Here goes:

(she sings)

AS I SIT HERE IN MY ROOM
TRYING TO THINK OF WHAT TO SAY
JUST ONE KID OUT OF SO MANY
AND YOU'RE OH, SO FAR AWAY
BEEN SO LONG SINCE I LAST WROTE
BUT THERE'S BEEN SO MUCH TO DO

AND I'VE TRIED THE VERY BEST THAT I COULD
TO DO WHAT MY PARENTS TELL ME I SHOULD
BUT FOR A GIRL LIKE ME IT'S NOT EASY TO BE
SO IMPOSSIBLY PERFECTLY GOOD

SO DEAR SANTA SINCE TOMORROW'S CHRISTMAS DAY
I GUESS WHAT I'M REALLY TRYING TO SAY IS...

I WOULDN'T MIND A NEW PAIR OF COWBOY BOOTS
OR A HORSE TO RIDE, OR A GUN THAT SHOOTS
NOT REAL, CAUSE I DON'T WANT TO HURT ANYONE
BUT I LOVE THE POP OF A GOOD POP GUN

I WOULDN'T MIND A BAT AND A BASEBALL GLOVE
AND A YANKEES HAT I WOULD REALLY LOVE
I USED TO PLAY SOCCER IN THE GRASS AND DIRT
BUT MY KNEES ARE STILL GREEN AND MY SHINS STILL HURT

SO IT'S PIRATE SHIPS AND 'LAND AHOY'
WOULDN'T MIND SOME SORT OF SWORD LIKE TOY
I'M A GIRL, THAT'S TRUE, BUT A GIRL CAN BE
AS TOUGH AS A BOY

I CAN RACE AND SLIDE AND CLIMB A TREE
NOT A BOY AROUND WHO'S FAST AS ME
AND I'LL BET I COULD BEAT 'EM ALL AT WII
IF YOU'VE GOT ONE IN YOUR BAG...

(spoken)

Just see!
CAUSE I HAVE A DOLL, NO I HAVE TEN
MOMMA BUYS THEM FOR ME AGAIN AND AGAIN
THERE'S THE EASY BAKE OVEN AND THE HAIR SALON
AND THE BARBIE STUFF JUST GOES ON AND ON
WITH THE RIBBONS AND THE BOWS AND THE PINK
CHIFFON
IT'S JUST I'M MORE JACK SPARROW THAN ELIZABETH SWAN

SO JUST KEEP IN MIND WHEN YOU READ MY LIST
IF IT'S PIRATE STUFF I JUST CAN'T RESIST
I WOULD RATHER BE THE HERO
THAN THE DAMSEL IN DISTRESS

STILL I WOULDN'T MIND WHATEVER YOU BRING
FOR I'M SURE YOU KNOW ALMOST EVERYTHING
AND BECAUSE I BELIEVE YOU'RE LISTENING
THERE IS SOMETHING I MUST STRESS
ON MY LIST YOU MAY THINK THERE'S SOMETHING'S WRONG
BUT IT'S NOT, IT'S THE REASON THAT I SANG THIS SONG
AND I'LL BET IT WON'T BE HARD FOR YOU TO GUESS

(spoken)

Let me put it this way.
A PIRATE NEVER, EVER WEARS A DRESS.

(spoken)

EVE. Thank you. Please keep this confidential.
Eve.

(**EVE** *climbs back into bed, closes her eyes and goes to sleep.*)

(*SFX: Wind TX: #3 **JOHNNY'S ENTRANCE***)

(*A wind starts to blow, as lights come up on a pirate flag billowing in the breeze.*)

(*Lightning crashes illuminating what is behind the flag. A **PIRATE** appears, crosses over to **EVE** and makes his way into the audience.*)

(*Music: #4 **SAIL ON***)

BLACK EYED JOHNNY. Avast, ye! They call me Black Eyed Johnny, and I'm the captain of this here vessel. We call 'er the Flyin' Dutchperson!

(*aside*)

These are PC times, ya' know.

(*and he's back*)

All of ye are stowaways on a journey to an island. The most famous island there is. Don't try figurin' it out, cause ya won't. Just sit back, swallow your grog, and pull alongside the hampers of the deep. Peer into the swollen, scaly eyes of the three headed sea monkey and join the fun. Come on, ye scalawags, we'll run a rig, we've just begun! Argh!

(*he sings*)

IF SAILOR TALES AND SAILOR TUNES
IF PIRATES, SCHOONERS AND DOUBLOONS
BUCCANEERS AND BURIED GOLD
BLOOD AND SWASH AND STORIES TOLD
IF YOU'VE A THIRST FOR GORE AND GRIME
THEN I'VE A TALE TO PASS THE TIME
SO GATHER ROUND, DON'T BREATHE A WORD
A STORY YOU HAVE NEVER HEARD
COME BOARD OUR SHIP WE'LL SAIL AWAY

(A group of pirates appear from different locations on the ship. They sing with **JOHNNY**.*)*

SAIL ON, SAIL ON, T' PLUNDER EVERY MILE
SAIL ON, SAIL ON, TO THE SANDS OF TREASURE ISLE

(In the distance the pirates see an Island. A beach.)

BLACK EYED JOHNNY. Avast ye! There she is blokes. The tropical island of all yer' dreams. All hands ahoy! Grab yer' tubes, and throw 'em overboard.

(A woman appears in a pool of light. This is **GRAINNE O'MALLY**, **BLACK EYED JOHNNY***'s wife. She is the* REAL *captain of the ship and she makes no bones about it.)*

GRAINNE O'MALLY. Ye heard 'im, you lazy picaroons. Get yer' lard into the water and paddle!

(The **PIRATES** *enter the sea wearing inner tubes. They begin to swim ashore.)*

BLACK EYED JOHNNY. Grainne O'Mally: I've told you once I've told you a billion times, I run this ship.

GRAINNE O'MALLY. Then stop posin' and run it before we plow the Dutchperson into those jagged rocks and kill us all.

(Everyone stops and looks to the stage [the jagged rocks], they take a deep "audible" gasp and let out a scream.)

EVERYONE. AHHHHHHH!

BLACK EYED JOHNNY. That's nothin'! We're not afraid of a little rocks, are we?

(The pirates respond [they are].)

BLACK EYED JOHNNY. Oh, come on, you blistering barnacles. It's right there beyond your eyes.

(he points)

Treasures untold and a'plenty! I can smell the doubloons from here.

PIRATES.
ASHORE, ASHORE, MAKE WAY, MAKE WAY

WE'RE PIRATES AND WE'VE COME TO TAKE THE BOOTY AND
    THE DAY
WE COME TO STEAL, LAY LOW, CLIMB HIGH AND SO WE GO
WE SPIN A TALE OF SKALYWAG, COME LISTEN AS WE BLOW

BLOW ASHORE, ASHORE, MAKE WAY, MAKE WAY
WE HAVE A JOB TO DO, BECAUSE WE'RE PIRATES JUST LIKE
    YOU
WE LIKE TO SWING AND JUMP AND FALL BACK ON OUR
    RUMP
THE OCEAN IS OUR HOME BUT LAND'S AHOY...

AHOY, AHOY, T' PLUNDER EVERY MILE
AHOY, AHOY, T' THE SANDS OF TREASURE ISLE

(The music continues as **TUSK**, **JOHNNY***'s sidekick, a
good natured pirate, broad smile and a twinkle in his
eye, cries out. His trusty parrot, Petey, perched on his
arm,* **TUSK** *is too tired to continue and he pauses in the
audience, out of breath.)*

TUSK. I don't think I can make it, Black Eyed Johnny. You'll
have to go on without me.

BLACK EYED JOHNNY. What're ye talkin' about?

TUSK. I can't swim.

(Another pirate, **WINKY**, *young and handsome, a bit of
a poser [likes the idea of being a pirate - the image - but
not the work], doesn't miss a beat.)*

WINKY. Don't worry about it, captain. I'll take his place.
That makes me number two, doesn't it? Look at me,
Pirate number two.
(to the audience)

How do I look? Do I look more important?

(He starts posing as the others watch, speechless.
GRAINNE *steps forward and grabs* **WINKY** *by the ear.)*

GRAINNE O'MALLY. No you don't look more important, you
look more ridiculous as if that was even possible. When
you have a man down who needs your help you don't
run over him, you pick him up and carry him. Didn't I
teach you anything? Where's your breeding, boy?

BLACK EYED JOHNNY. Enough, enough! Tusk, don't be daft. Just hold onto your tube and you'll be fine. All of ye, just keep floatin'.
And if you start to fail...

(he looks into the audience)

...just ask one of these seals to help you.

*(**TUSK** asks one of the children from the audience to help him.)*

(All of the pirates follow suit and start failing, and asking help from the audience.)

(A girl pirate enters the water, also wearing an inner tube.)

RUBY RED. Weigh anchor! Hoist the mitsen!

EVERYONE. MIZEN!

RUBY RED. Whatever!

*(From behind **RUBY RED** comes **JIMMY JACK** [a child pirate in training]. He runs in and starts swinging on the rope. He is followed by **JUNKMAN JAKE**, a Scottish pirate who speaks in broken Scottish.)*

JIMMY JACK. Wait for me! I'm comin'. All hands at sea!

JUNKMAN. Ah dinnae ken whir me haggis az. *(I don't know where my haggis is.)*

(The rest of the crew crawl through the audience and land on a rock a few feet from land. [They are, however, still in the audience])

(They sing.)

EVERYONE.
ASHORE, ASHORE, MAKE WAY, MAKE WAY
THERE'S TREASURES THERE FOR TAKIN'
AND WE'RE MAKIN' MORE THAN HAY
WE'RE ON A QUEST, A COUP, A JOURNEY JUST LIKE YOU
THE OCEAN IS OUR HOME BUT LAND'S AHOY...

EVERYONE.

> AHOY, AHOY, T' PLUNDER EVERY MILE
> AHOY, AHOY, AS WE LAND ON TREASURE ISLE
>
> *(They all meet at the foot of the stage and encounter a whirlpool.)*
>
> *(Sound: TX: #5 **WHIRLPOOL FX**)*
>
> *(choreographed movement of the crew being tossed around, almost falling off the rock.)*

BLACK EYED JOHNNY. We'll have to swing over the whirlpool, mates. Who wants to go first?

WINKY. I'll go last.

BLACK EYED JOHNNY. I'll go LAST? I said, who wants to go first?

> *(Nothing. **JOHNNY** calls them into a huddle.)*

BLACK EYED JOHNNY. Alright, here's what we'll do.

> *(indicating the audience)*

We'll get one of them to try it first and make sure it's safe. That way if they fall into the whirlpool, we only lose an audience member, not an actor.

> *(The **PIRATES** slowly and menacingly look out at the audience.)*
>
> *(**WINKY** jumps away from the pirates and starts combing the audience looking for a willing participant.)*

WINKY. I'll find 'em, Johnny. Alright, who wants to swing over the whirlpool to Treasure Island?

> *(This is a fun moment of audience participation. Try to find a child who clearly wants to be on stage.)*
>
> *(**WINKY** returns with the recruit. He stands him in front of **JOHNNY**.)*

BLACK EYED JOHNNY. What's your name, lad?

> *(the child answers)*

That's a good name, but it doesn't sound very piratey. What's your pirate name?

(if the child doesn't come up with one, let the group name him or her.)

Alright, *(Name)*, on the count of three, you're goin' to swing across this here rope, over the whirlpool, and onto Treasure Island. Do you think you can do that?

(He waits for an answer and then cheers the audience on in support.)

That's me boy *(or gal)*. On the count of three. Got it? Alright, here we go. ONE...TWO...

(Just as the person is about to try it, GRAINNE steps up and stops them.)

GRAINNE O'MALLY. *(to the audience member)* Wait a minute! We can't let you do it.

EVERYONE. WHY NOT?

GRAINNE O'MALLY. Our insurance won't cover it.

PIRATES. AWW!

BLACK EYED JOHNNY. Well, lad, don't ya go feelin' bad. I have somethin' here for you to say thanks for even takin' the challenge.

(he pulls out a whistle)

This is a special whistle for you to use a little later in the show. We'll be needin' your help, so you hold onto this and we'll tell you when to use it. Can you do that?

(The PIRATES all pat the child on the back, returning him/her, to his/her seat.)

BLACK EYED JOHNNY. Alright! One of us has to go. Who's it gonna be?

(JIMMY JACK steps forward and with a flurry of bravado he grabs the rope and declares...)

JIMMY JACK. I'll do it!

(JIMMY JACK swings over the rock and lands perfectly on the shore. He bows for the audience.)

RUBY RED. Well, if a little boy can do it. I certainly can do it!

(She swings effortlessly onto the shore.)

(A pirate steps up and speaks. She is unintelligible.)

JUNKMAN JAKE. Ah dunaekin whee afee wee bonny barin laddy kindaeit, whee noot micell-like? *(I don't know why, if a cute little kid can do it…why not me?)*

(JOHNNY *and* **GRAINNE** *look to one another.)*

GRAINNE O'MALLY. I have no idea what she just said.

(JUNKMAN *swings across the rope and lands on the island.)*

(TUSK *steps forward. [He has a parrot attached to his wrist - this is Petey].)*

TUSK. Well, if a little boy, a girl, and an unintelligible Scottsperson can do it. Petey and I can certainly do it!

(to Petey)

Flap your wings hard Petey!

(TUSK *makes it across, but barely. He is shook up at how hard it was.)*

(WINKY *steps up, grabs the rope and then backs down.)*

BLACK EYED JOHNNY. Oh, for the love of Hogshead! *(to* **WINKY***)* Get across before I throw you into the whirlpool m'self.

(GRAINNE *steps up, grabs the rope.)*

GRAINNE O'MALLY. Here! Watch and learn lad. Watch and learn!

(She spits on her hands, grabs the rope again with mighty intention, and throws it to the others to catch.)

When you can't swing…you swim.

(GRAINNE *plunges into the water, gets caught up in the whirlpool and pulls herself out [the others helping her along the way].)*

(Upon reaching shore, she lets out a gasp of relief.)

GRAINNE O'MALLY. Ahhhhh! That was refreshin'. I'm still hot, but it only comes in flashes.

WINKY. *(applauding)* Granny, that was wonderful!

GRAINNE O'MALLY. GRAINNE! Not Granny. I'm nobody's Granny! Now get over here so I can knock some sense into that monkey head of yers.

WINKY. Well, if a little boy, a girl, an unintelligible Scottsperson, a clown with a parrot...

(under his breath)

...and a granny can do it...

GRAINNE O'MALLY. I heard that!

WINKY. Surely I can do it.

*(**BLACK EYED JOHNNY** throws him at the rope and he swings across, screaming all the way. He misses the rock, and swings back over the audience, almost taking **BLACK EYED JOHNNY** out in the process.)*

WINKY. AHHHHHHHHHHHHHHHH!

*(Finally, he makes it safe across the whilrpool, being pulled into safety by **GRAINNE**.)*

Thank you Grainne! I owe ye' me life.

GRAINNE O'MALLY. Find somethin' more valuable, then we'll talk.

BLACK EYED JOHNNY. Alright, now let me show you scalawags the way it's done!

*(**BLACK EYED JOHNNY** swings with a little too much energy, misses the deck and lands back on the rock with a thud.)*

TUSK. That had to hurt!

*(Finally, with the help of the audience, **JOHNNY** makes it across the whirlpool.)*

(Once they reach the stage, they are immediately struck with the freezing weather.)

*(TX: #6 **COLD WIND**)*

GRAINNE O'MALLY. The weather's gone bonkers. It's crackin' me cheeks.

BLACK EYED JOHNNY. Someone get me me coat.

JIMMY JACK. We left it on the ship, sir.

RUBY RED. We've never needed coats before. What's happening?

TUSK. Maybe it's global warming.

BLACK EYED JOHNNY. Global what?

TUSK. *(referring to the parrot)* Petey heard it on CNN.

*(**JOHNNY** lets out a scream and looks up into the sky as a few flurries of snow begin to fall from above.)*

*(Music: TX: #7 **SNOW**)*

(They have never seen snow before and they all react as though they are being attacked by aliens. Swords come out, some of them fighting with the snowflakes …it's pandemonium.)

BLACK EYED JOHNNY. What was that?

TUSK. What was what?

BLACK EYED JOHNNY. That thing...that white thing that hit me.

GRAINNE O'MALLY. What white thing that hit you? I don't see any white thing...AHHHHH!

*(**GRAINNE** screams from the feeling she gets when a piece of snow hits her.)*

BLACK EYED JOHNNY. There, you see. What did I tell you.

(They all look up and see the sky start opening up with snow. They have NEVER seen snow before!)

*(**JOHNNY** sings…)*

BLACK EYED JOHNNY.
WHAT'S THIS, IT'S WET, IT'S COLD, IT'S WHITE
IT GLISTEN'S AND IT SHINES
AND YET THERE'S SOMETHING JUST NOT RIGHT
CAUSE IT'S THERE, THEN IT'S NOT
OH BEWARE, THERE'S SOMETHING ROTTEN

GRAINNE O'MALLY.

LOOK, IT'S MELTED ON ME NOSE

WINKY.

OH DEAR, I CAN'T FEEL ME TOES

EVERYONE.

FROZEN FINGERS, FROZEN TOES

(Everyone looks up, screams, continues singing.)

EVERYONE.

WHAT'S THIS, HOW STRANGE, IT LANDS, THEN GOES
IT'S FLAKY AND IT'S SMALL

GRAINNE O'MALLY.

AND NOW IT'S UP INSIDE ME HOSE

EVERYONE.

IT ATTACKS, I CAN'T SEE
IT REACTS INSIDE OF ME
OH THERE'S AN ALIEN INSIDE
AND THERE'S NOWHERE LEFT TO HIDE

HEAVEN KNOWS WHERE WE'VE LANDED
WE'RE ALL STRANDED ON THIS ICE
THOUGH IT LOOKS A BIT LIKE COTTON
OR THIS WEIRD ROBOTIC RICE
IN FACT...IT COULD...BE LICE

*(They all react to the idea of lice being inside their body
and start scratching and screaming.)*

EVERYONE.

WHAT'S THIS, IT FLITS, IT PUFFS, IT FLIES
GETS SLICK AND STICKS TOGETHER

TUSK.

THEN IT CAKES AROUND ME EYES

EVERYONE.

MAKES ME WHEEZE, MAKES ME SNEEZE
IT'S LIKE FEATHERS ON A BREEZE

WINKY.

I'LL BET THIS STUFF SNUFFED OUT THE TREES

EVERYONE.

> GET ME OUT OF THIS PLACE PLEASE
> IT'S NOT RIGHT

BLACK EYED JOHNNY.

> IT'S ALL SO WHITE

EVERYONE.

> AND IT'S BLINDING IT'S SO BRIGHTENING
> IT'S FRIGHTENING
> IT'S THE WATER FROM THE SKY...CURSE

BLACK EYED JOHNNY. *(spoken)* Me Mum told me about it when I was a wee lad. She said it only happened when someone's really bad...like telling lies or cheating, or stealing from a friend...or prayin' to Davy Jones to save yer bones at the world's end!

(really losin' it)

WHICH IS WHERE WE ARE RIGHT NOW!

EVERYONE.

> WE'RE HERE, FOR NOW, IT'S CLEAR SOMEHOW
> WE MUST KNOW WHERE WE ARE
> TO KNOW WHICH WAY TO TURN OUR BOW
> ALL THIS ICE ISN'T NICE
> AND WE'RE SURE TO PAY TH' PRICE
> AND MY ADVICE IS MAN THE SHIP
> CAUSE ME TONGUE'S FROZE TO ME LIP!

*(The **PIRATES** stick their tongues onto their swords to check the temperature. Their tongues freeze onto their swords. [They sing the next line with their tongues on the swords].)*

FROZEN FINGERS, FROZEN TOES
HEAVEN KNOWS WHERE WE'VE ALL LANDED

(They pull the swords from their tongues. Pain.)

STRANDED...
IT'S THE WATER FROM THE SKY...CURSE!
WE'RE IN TROUBLE
IT'S THE WATER FROM THE SKY...CURSE!
SOMEONE HELP US

OFF THIS GODFORSAKEN, BODY SHAKEN
COURSE WE'VE TAKEN, WORST MISTAKEN
PLACE WE'VE EVER BEEN
IT COULDN'T GET MUCH WORSE
IT'S THE WATER FROM THE SKY CURSE

(*The* **PIRATES** *all scream and collapse.*)

BLACK EYED JOHNNY. (*to* **TUSK**) Tusk! Are you sure you had the coordinates correct? This don't feel like Treasure Isle. Tropical, sunny, HOT! I'll hang you from the hempin' halter if you took us on the wrong path again.

TUSK. No, Black Eyed Johnny. I followed the map precisely.

BLACK EYED JOHNNY. Well, where in the name of Rocky Bottom are we?

(**RUBY RED** *reads a sign hanging on the dock.*)

RUBY RED. We're at Eloph Tron.

BLACK EYED JOHNNY. Where?

RUBY RED. (*pointing to the sign*) Eloph Tron.

JIMMY JACK. That's not what it says.

RUBY RED. Yes it does.

(*reading the sign*)

Eloph Tron.

BLACK EYED JOHNNY. Ruby Red, how many times do I have to tell you that you have to read from top to bottom, or from left to right.

(*to the audience*)

Ever since we travelled to Singapore she reads things backwards.

(*to* **RUBY RED**)

Move out of the way, you varmint ye'.

(*He tries to read the sign and cannot. He mispronounces it badly, ending in...*)

BLACK EYED JOHNNY. Nor-te-huh Pol-eyee...

TUSK. I think it's French!

BLACK EYED JOHNNY. Jimmy Jack...what does that say?

JIMMY JACK. North Pole.

BLACK EYED JOHNNY. Blunderin' shellfish, where the devil did you take us, Tusk?

JIMMY JACK. To the North Pole. I just said that.

RUBY RED. And I'm FREEZING.

WINKY. And I'm startin' to feel a little dizzy.

TUSK. How can you tell?

WINKY. What does that mean?

TUSK. You're always dizzy...

(The **PIRATES** *all weigh in on* **WINKY***'s dizziness.* **GRAINNE** *steps in.)*

GRAINNE O'MALLY. Alright, there's no need in throwin' yer' spirits into the bilge over it.

JUNKMAN JAKE. Ats bither af yoos chillax. Dunnt git all humpty-like. *(It's better if you chill and relax. Don't get upset.)*

GRAINNE O'MALLY. Right! Tusk, where's the map?

BLACK EYED JOHNNY. *(to* **GRAINNE***)* Excuse me! I'll ask him where's the map.

GRAINNE O'MALLY. Then ask him.

BLACK EYED JOHNNY. I will.

GRAINNE O'MALLY. Now!

BLACK EYED JOHNNY. Tusk, where's the map?

TUSK. I followed the map perfectly, I did. Look!

*(***TUSK** *takes out a map and lays it on the stage. They all gather round and look at the map, crowding* **BLACK EYED JOHNNY** *out of the way.)*

BLACK EYED JOHNNY. Give us some room, ye cackle fruit.

TUSK. Cackle fruit? What's that mean?

BLACK EYED JOHNNY. It means you're as raw as a bunch of hen's eggs.

TUSK. Why don't you just say that, then?

BLACK EYED JOHNNY. Get out of me way.

(**BLACK EYED JOHNNY** *reads the map. He ponders it…
turns his head this way and that. He steps back and
tries to make sense of it with his sword, looking at how
the sun hits the ground. Everyone ooh's and ahh's as he
does his work.*)

(*Finally…after much posing, he walks slowly up to the
map, turns it around and looks over at* **TUSK**.)

TUSK. Uh Oh!

BLACK EYED JOHNNY. Ye had it upside down you miserable
little water vermin.

TUSK. I'm sorry.

PETEY. Anyone can make a mistake, Black Eyed Johnny.

RUBY RED. Yeah, no need to get all ornery about it. Let's
just buck up and see what's happening on this island.

WINKY. There must be someone here we can loot.

(*They look around, jumping up and down the levels to
see what they can see.*)

BLACK EYED JOHNNY. Ahoy, Matey! Anyone here?

(*They listen…nothing.*)

RUBY RED. Maybe they're hiding.

TUSK. They might have seen us when we landed.

JIMMY JACK. I'm ready for 'em.

(*yelling*)

Argh!

BLACK EYED JOHNNY. That's nice, Jimmy Jack. Save it for
later.

RUBY RED. (*to* **BLACK EYED JOHNNY**) Captain, should we
run a shot across the bow (*mispronounced*) and see who
comes a runnin'?

EVERYONE. BOW!

(**RUBY** *takes a bow.*)

BLACK EYED JOHNNY. (*incredulous*) You wanna swim back
out there and shoot the cannons?

RUBY RED. Well, I just thought...

BLACK EYED JOHNNY. Cause that was a long swim.

TUSK. Very long.

GRAINNE O'MALLY. Then what're we gonna do? Come about and spit it out if ye have somethin' floatin' around in that little head of yers.

BLACK EYED JOHNNY. Let's split up, cover the island. If you find anything, use your whistle and let us know. We'll find you out. Just keep whistling.

(grabbing his whistle)

Let's practice.

(to the child from the audience with the whistle)

You too *(child's pirate name)*. Take out your whistle and join us.

(They all grab their whistles and start whistling.)

*(**JUNKMAN JAKE**, upset about something, runs over to **JOHNNY** and starts spouting out unintelligible words.)*

JUNKMAN JAKE. Ah dunaekin whirrr me blawy-tingy as. Ah loost me whustly. Geey's a han. *(I don't know where my whistle is. I lost my whistle. Help me.)*

BLACK EYED JOHNNY. What is it Junkman? What're ye' tryin' to tell me.

JUNKMAN JAKE. Wit migone t'dae? Whin ah fee t'bampot what nicked me blawy-tingy, ah'll stoat der wallies. *(What am I going to do? When I find out the crazy person who took my whistle, I'll punch them in the teeth.)*

GRAINNE O'MALLY. Slow down, lad.

JUNKMAN JAKE. Ah wiz fleeing crass, gaun ower, muckin' aboot, n soom radge winday-licker nicked me blawyt-ingy. No ats dassapeerrrdth.. *(I was flying across, going over, messing about and some crazy fool stole my whistle. Now it's disappeared.)*

GRAINNE O'MALLY. *(understanding)* She doesn't have her whistle. *(beat)* She lost it swimmin' across the whirlpool.

(*JOHNNY hands her a spare whistle. She smiles and walks away.*)

JUNKMAN JAKE. Tanks!

BLACK EYED JOHNNY. Alright...let's go. Tusk, Winky...you go that way. Ruby, Junkman...that way. Grainne...over the hill.

(**GRAINNE** *gives him a look.*)

And Jimmy Jack, you're comin' with me.

(*They all start to go. He stops them.*)

And remember! Whistle if you see something.

(*to audience*)

You too. If you see anything, whistle. Try it. Let's hear.

(*The audience whistles.*)

BLACK EYED JOHNNY. Shiver me' timbers. We have ourselves a lookout squad. (*to the others*) Let's go men!

(*Everyone begins to run off.* **RUBY** *remembers something.*)

RUBY RED. What about the shield?

TUSK. We always forget the shield. What's that about? Why do we always forget the shield.

WINKY. WE don't always forget the shield. YOU are in charge of the shield. YOU are the one who forgets. Nobody else...Yooooooouuuuu!

GRAINNE O'MALLY. Oh, enough already, why don't ye just...

(*she looks at* **JOHNNY** *and stops*)

BLACK EYED JOHNNY. (*yelling, holding it out for what seems like forever*) ENOUGH!

(*The pirates find this display impressive and begin to applaud.* **JOHNNY** *takes their applause with grace and humility.*)

Tusk...the shield.

(**TUSK** *comes to the edge of the shore and pulls out a gadget that he points to the ship. [This should be the sound of a car alarm being set])*

*(TX: #8 **THE SHIELD** #1)*

PIRATES. Ahhhhhh!

BLACK EYED JOHNNY. Alright Pirates...let's see what The North Pole has in store for us.

(They exit. [This should be a choreographed exit timed to the music.])

*(TX: #9 **SAIL ON PLAYOFF - EVE'S ENTRANCE**)*

(From behind a wall, a little girl's face emerges. She is all dressed in a red outfit and wearing a hat and gloves, a scarf and mufflers.)

(The audience is probably now whistling loudly.)

*(She runs out to the audience and tells them not to whistle. This is **EVE CHRISTMAS**. She is the daughter to the head of the Elves, **MURRAY** and **HAPPY CHRISTMAS**. [and the little girl from the opening])*

EVE. Don't whistle. Don't whistle.

(to audience)

Did you see those Pirates? What did they want?
(she listens to the audience)

Well, they don't belong here. I can tell you that. It's Christmas eve and I don't think Santa will be happy about this.

(she sees their pirate ship in the distance)

Look! There's their pirate ship. And it's starting to disappear.
(calling off)

Mommy! Daddy! Come quick! Hurry!

*(Eve's parents, **HAPPY** and **MURRAY CHRISTMAS** come running around the corner. They are followed by their older daughters, **HOLLY** & **IVY**.)*

HAPPY. Eve, what is it?

MURRAY. What's the matter, sweetheart?

EVE. Look! A pirate ship.

> *(TX: #10 **SHIP DISAPPEARS**)*

> *(They all look out at the ocean. They don't see anything.)*

EVE. Oh my goodness. It's vanished.

> *(The **GIRLS** laugh at their sister and her silliness.)*

HAPPY. *(to the **GIRLS**)* Alright, alright. No laughing at your sister.

MURRAY. *(laughing)* You have quite an imagination, young elf. You should become a writer.

EVE. But it was right there. I saw it.

HOLLY. Well, it's not there now.

EVE. There are pirates on the North Pole. I just saw them.

IVY. Pirates?

HAPPY. Sweetie. There are no such things as pirates any more.

MURRAY. They're only in the movies.

HOLLY. Yeah, like Captain Jack Sparrow.

HOLLY & IVY. *(dreamy)* We love him.

MURRAY. But he's only in the movies. He's not landing at the North Pole.

HOLLY. You never know.

EVE. *(to the audience)* But I saw them. They were standing right here and they were singing.

HAPPY. Singing pirates?

IVY. What were they singing?

HOLLY. There's no such thing as singing pirates.

EVE. I'll prove it to you.

> *(to the audience)*

> If you saw pirates...yell PIRATES.

> *(The audience yells to the stage.)*

> *(**MURRAY** and **HAPPY** come down and talk to the audience.)*

(*Music: TX: #11* ***WHERE ARE THEY NOW?***)

MURRAY. So you all saw pirates, did you?

HAPPY. What did they look like?

(*As the audience yells out their answers, the family of elves interact with them. At a specific point in the music,* **MURRAY** *begins to sing.*)

MURRAY.

DID THEY HAVE BIG HATS WITH SWORDS A SLICIN'

HAPPY.

DID THEY CARRY BATS, DID THEY FLY A BISON

HOLLY & IVY.

WERE THEY YO, HO, HO'IN

HAPPY.

AND JUST WHERE WERE THEY GOIN'

ALL FOUR.

AND IF YOU BELIEVE IN PIRATES
THEN JUST WHERE ARE THEY NOW

EVE. I don't know where they are. But they were standing right here on this beach.

(*to audience*)

Weren't they?

HOLLY & IVY.

DID THEY WEAR A PATCH OVER ONE OF THEIR EYES
DID THEY HAVE PEG LEGS, CARRY GUNS ON THEIR THIGHS

HAPPY.

DID THEY BRING ALONG A PLANK

HOLLY & IVY.

WHAT ABOUT THEIR SHIP

EVE.

IT SANK

MURRAY. That's right, she did say that.

ALL FOUR.

WE DON'T MEAN TO POKE FUN

HAPPY.

BUT HON...

ALL FOUR.

> WHERE ARE THEY NOW

EVE. I don't know. I told you, they ran off.

ALL FOUR.

> WHERE ARE THEY NOW, WHERE ARE THEY NOW
> WE DON'T SEE 'EM, WE DON'T HEAR 'EM

MURRAY.

> AND I, FOR ONE, DON'T FEAR 'EM
> WHY IF THEY WERE HERE I'D FIGHT 'EM TO THE BOW

EVERYONE.

> WHERE ARE THEY NOW, WHERE ARE THEY NOW

HAPPY.

> IN A PUFF OF SMOKE THEY VANISH

HOLLY.

> WERE THEY FRENCH

IVY.

> OR MAYBE SPANISH

MURRAY & HAPPY.

> DOESN'T MATTER, THEY'RE NOT HERE

ALL FOUR.

> ANYHOW, THEY'RE NOT HERE NOW.

EVE. But they were here, I'm telling you.

HAPPY. Honey, you're just excited about Christmas. And your little elf mind is working overtime, that's all.

EVE. No, that's not it.

HAPPY.

> IT'S IN YOUR IMAGINATION

MURRAY.

> NOT IN ROCK OR VEGETATION

ALL FOUR.

> YOU'VE IMAGINED QUITE A STORY AND IT'S FUN

HAPPY.

> BUT LOOK AROUND, WHAT DO YOU SEE
> THERE'S NOT PIRATES

ALL FOUR.

> ONLY ME...ONLY ME...ONLY ME

MURRAY.

NOW COME ALONG

HAPPY.

IT'S CHRISTMAS EVE

HOLLY & IVY.

THERE'S LOTS TO DO

ALL FOUR.

WE'VE GOT TO RUN

EVE. But I saw them. I did! I really did.

HAPPY. But sweetheart, look around.

ALL FOUR.

WHERE ARE THEY NOW, WHERE ARE THEY NOW

MURRAY.

NO MORE TALKING, SANTA NEEDS US

HAPPY.

HE'S THE MAN WHO CLOTHES AND FEEDS US

HOLLY & IVY.

AND THERE'S TOYS TO WRAP

MURRAY.

AND REINDEER POOP TO PLOW

(Everyone stops and looks at **MURRAY**.*)*

MURRAY. What? That's my job. Cleaning up the reindeer poop.

HOLLY. Too much information!

IVY. Way!

HAPPY. Nonsense! He should be very proud of his position. It's a darn good job. Someone has to do it.

MURRAY. And it's me...MURRAY CHRISTMAS.

EVE. Does anyone even care about the pirates?

EVERYONE.

WHERE ARE THEY NOW

(The song ends with a flourish a la the old movie musicals. **EVE** *just looks at her family in disbelief.)*

EVE. You don't believe me.

HOLLY & IVY. That's what we've been saying.

EVE. But I'm telling you. They all ran off in different directions.

MURRAY. Honey, this is the North Pole. Where could they have gone? We would have seen them.

HAPPY. It's Christmas Eve, sweetie. We have a lot of work to do. Santa's not feeling well and the reindeer are all sneezing and coughing.

MURRAY. Why don't we go back to Santa's workshop and help the other elves load the sleigh.

EVE. But I saw them. I really did.

(The **PIRATES** *all enter from above, sneaking onto the stage. We play a little game of FREEZE and MOVE.*)

(*The audience at this point is probably whistling and the family of elves can play with them, turning and pretending not to see the pirates. This goes on until* **MURRAY** *decides he's had enough.*)

MURRAY. (*to* HAPPY) Maybe we should listen to them and send out a team of scouts to see if anyone did land on the island.

HAPPY. (*to* MURRAY) Oh, fiddle-de-dee. This is all just part of Christmas nervousness. Remember the Christmas you thought you saw a flying saucer?

MURRAY. I DID see a flying saucer.

HAPPY. But no one else did.

HOLLY. I saw a giant sea-horse once.

EVERYONE. We all saw that!

HOLLY. I know. I'm just saying I saw one.

EVE. This is different. You have to believe me. I think they're gonna do something terrible.

HAPPY. Honey, I want you to listen to me. There are no such things as pirates. And nothing terrible is going to happen on Christmas Isle.

MURRAY. Santa wouldn't let it. And neither would I. So don't you worry. Everything will be just fine.

HAPPY. Now, we'd all better get back to the workshop.

(**HOLLY** *sneaks over to* **EVE** *and torments her.* **IVY** *follows.*)

HOLLY. Arrgh! The ghost of Davy Jones'll be comin' for ye', ye' filthy wench. Givin' us up like that.

IVY. Ooh! That was really good. Say it again, say it again.

HAPPY. Alright, enough of that you two. We have work to do.

MURRAY. Holly! Ivy! Come along!

HAPPY. Eve?

EVE. I'll be right there.

(*Everyone exits.*)

(*TX: #12* ***WHERE ARE THEY NOW? PLAYOFF***)

(**EVE** *stays onstage, looking out at the audience. She talks to them.*)

EVE. Maybe they're right. Maybe it was just my imagination.

(*The* **PIRATES** *jump down from the rocks and surround Eve.*)

PIRATES. AARGH!

(*She doesn't budge, pretending not to see or hear them. They try again.*)

PIRATES. AARGH!

(*Still nothing. They all react.*)

BLACK EYED JOHNNY. Aren't you gonna scream or somethin'?

EVE. (*looking right at* **JOHNNY**) You don't exist.

BLACK EYED JOHNNY. What dya' mean, I don't exist?

EVE. You're just in my mind.

GRAINNE O'MALLY. We are not in your mind. We're on your beach.

RUBY RED. And we've got all your toys.

BLACK EYED JOHNNY. Wait a mariner's minute. What dya' mean, tellin' me I don't exist. I could make ya walk the plank for sayin' somethin' like that, you slimy little eel, you.

EVE. I am not slimy and I'm not an eel. I'm an elf!

WINKY. Did she say elk?

TUSK. No, she said Elf. You know, those little guys in the trees who bake cookies?

WINKY. Cookies? You mean she's a Girl Scout?

(*The* **PIRATES** *all ad lib cookie orders for different types of Girl Scout cookies.*)

EVE. I am NOT a Girl Scout. I'm an ELF!

BLACK EYED JOHNNY. Tie her up. We're takin' her with us.

JUNKMAN JAKE. Ah goat a jute. While cordit t weain. (*I got a rope. We'll tie up the kid*)

RUBY RED. But why are we takin' her with us? What can she do for us?

(*The* **PIRATES** *form a circle around* **EVE,** *leaning in asking her the following questions.*)

BLACK EYED JOHNNY. Can you cook?

EVE. No.

PIRATES. Argh!

TUSK. Can you clean?

EVE. No.

PIRATES. Argh!

RUBY RED. Can you sew?

EVE. No.

PIRATES. Argh!

BLACK EYED JOHNNY. Well, shiver me' timbers, lass, what can you do?

EVE. I can SCREAM.

(**EVE** *starts to scream. The* **PIRATES** *all drop their bags and hold their hands over their ears.*)

(**MRS. SANTA** *comes running through the* **PIRATES** *and grabs* **EVE.***)*

MRS. SANTA. What's going on here? *(looking at the bags)* Where did you get these bags? These are Santa's bags. You have no business carrying these bags. Put them down at once. They have to be loaded onto the sled.

GRAINNE O'MALLY. They're bein' loaded...

(JOHNNY motions to GRAINNE to STOP TALKIN'! He then turns to MRS. SANTA and repeats her very words.)

BLACK EYED JOHNNY. They're bein' loaded onto our Pirate ship. *(to TUSK)* Tusk. Lower the shield.

(TUSK pulls out his gadget and drops the shield from the pirate ship.)

*(TX: #13 **THE SHIELD #2**)*

EVE. There it is. I knew I saw it. I knew it.

MRS. SANTA. *(to JOHNNY)* How did you get all the way up here?

RUBY RED. Tusk had the map upside down.

MRS. SANTA. Well, I'm sorry, but you'll have to give those bags back. They have to be delivered to all the boys and girls around the world tonight. What would Christmas be without presents for all the little boys and girls.

(Beat)

BLACK EYED JOHNNY. Who are you?

MRS. SANTA. I'm Mrs. Santa Claus.

*(A flourish of lights and music accompany the recognition of **MRS. SANTA CLAUS**.)*

*(TX: #14 **MRS. CLAUSE #1**)*

BLACK EYED JOHNNY. Mrs. who?

MRS. SANTA. *(annoyed)* Mrs. Santa Claus.

(Repeat of lights and music.)

*(TX: #15 **MRS. CLAUSE #2**)*

TUSK. Doesn't ring a bell.

MRS. SANTA. You've never heard of Santa Claus?

BLACK EYED JOHNNY. Does he have a pirate ship?

MRS. SANTA. No.

BLACK EYED JOHNNY. Then we never heard of him.

> *(stepping in to Mrs. Claus)*

> Can you cook?

EVE. Say no.

MRS. SANTA. Yes.

PIRATES. Score!

TUSK. Can you clean?

EVE. Say no.

MRS. SANTA. Yes.

PIRATES. Score!

RUBY RED. Can you sew?

EVE. Say NO.

MRS. SANTA. No.

PIRATES. Awe!

MRS. SANTA. *(to audience)* I really can't.

BLACK EYED JOHNNY. *(to the* **PIRATES***)* Tie 'em up. We'll take em' both with us.

> *(The* **PIRATES** *approach* **EVE** *and* **MRS. SANTA.** **EVE** *starts screaming again.)*

> *(MUSIC: TX: #16* **THE CHASE***)*

> *(They try to stop her but she runs them ragged.)*

> *(This is intended to be a Keystone Cops-like chase throughout the theatre.)*

> *(***MURRAY, HAPPY, HOLLY** *and* **IVY** *enter.)*

> *(A choreographed fight ensues. The* **PIRATES** *pull their swords, but the* **ELVES** *have other weapons up their sleeves [such as all different types of toys].)*

> *(They all go off in different directions.)*

> *(A snowman is pushed on stage.)*

> *(***EVE** *enters and looks around. She talks to the audience.)*

EVE. Where did they go?

(The audience talks back to her.)

(We hear the **PIRATES** *coming from the distance.* **EVE** *hides behind the snowman.)*

*(***TUSK*** enters, talking to his parrot,* **PETEY**. **WINKY** *follows behind.)*

PETEY. I told you not to get lost.

TUSK. I am not lost.

PETEY. You're always lost.

TUSK. Stop talking. I can't hear myself think.

PETEY. Then stop thinking so you can hear me talk.

*(***WINKY*** enters, sees the snowman and screams. He then runs over to* **TUSK** *and jumps in his arms.)*

WINKY. What is it?

TUSK. It's a water from the sky person.

WINKY. What should we do?

PETEY. Why don't you go over there and say hello.

*(***PETEY*** flies over to* **EVE**.*)*

Hello!

EVE. *(pretending to be the snowman)* Hello!

WINKY. Blisterin' Barnicles, it talks.

TUSK. *(getting it)* Wait a minute. You sound an awful lot like that little girl. What was her name?

WINKY. Morning/Afternoon

TUSK. AM/PM

WINKY. Dawn/Dusk!

PETEY. Eve!

TUSK. Eve! Come out from behind that...thing.

*(***EVE*** crosses from behind the snowman.)*

WINKY. I knew that's who was back there.

EVE. Really? Then why did you scream.

WINKY. To throw you off the track.

EVE. Right!

TUSK. Alright, let's just get her and take her back to Black Eyed Johnny.

*(**TUSK** starts to cross to **EVE** but **PETEY** pulls him back.)*

TUSK. Petey, what's wrong with you? Let's go?

*(Again, **PETEY** puls him back.)*

WINKY. Oh for the love of Neptune.

TUSK. Petey! What's gotten into you?

PETEY. Gi'me your ear.

TUSK. I will not give you my ear. Last time you almost swallowed it.

WINKY. He swallowed your ear? He doesn't have a mouth. Have you noticed that? It doesn't open. Hello?

PETEY. Hello!

WINKY. Stop doing that.

EVE. *(to **PETEY**)* What's the matter Petey? What do you want? You can tell Evie.

*(Music: TX: #17 **PETEY'S SONG**)*

PETEY. Evie...that's a pretty name.

EVE. Thank you Petey. I like your name too. So what can we do for you?

PETEY.

PETEY WANT TO EAT SOME CRACKERS

TUSK.

THERE'S NO TIME TO THINK ABOUT PETEY

PETEY.

FRUITS AND NUTS AND SEEDS AND SNACKERS

TUSK.

PETEY TENDS TO BE QUITE NEEDY

PETEY.

PETEY LIKE THE GIRL NAMED EVIE

TUSK.

SHE DON'T HAVE NO CRUMB FOR PETEY

PETEY.

PETEY GET MAD, PETEY WANT BAD

WINKY.

    PETEY'S A PAIN IN THE...FEATHERS!

TUSK. Come on, Petey, we have to take her back to Johnny before...

PETEY. Let her go!

WINKY. *(to* **PETEY***)* No, we can't let her go. *(to* **TUSK***)* Will you stop talkin' to yourself. Black Eyed Johnny will be here any minute and if we don't have her tied up and ready...

PETEY.

    PETEY LIKE TO BITE ON NOSES

TUSK.

    PETEY'S BEAK CAN BE ANNOYING

PETEY.

    PETEY LIKE TO POOP ON CLOTHESES

TUSK.

    ALL MY WARDROBE HE'S DESTROYING

WINKY.

    WE CAN'T LET HIM STOP THIS CAPER

    HOW 'BOUT PARROT SOUP FOR DINNER

PETEY.

    PETEY GET ROUGH, PETEY REAL TOUGH

EVE.

    I THINK PETEY'S QUITE...CHARMING

PETEY.

    SHE THINKS PETEY'S QUITE CHARMING

    *(***TUSK*** is suddenly pulled around the stage by a flying* **PETEY***.)*

PETEY.

    PETEY WANT TO HELP SAVE EVIE

WINKY.

    THAT IS NOT SO GOOD FOR WINKIE

TUSK.

    NOW YOU'RE MAKING ME GET PEEVIE

PETEY.

    KEEP IT UP, YOUR HEADS I'LL SHRINKIE

TUSK.

YOU DON'T SCARE ME

WINKY.

YOU DON'T FRIGHTEN

PETEY.

EVER FELT A PARROT BITIN'

TUSK & WINKIE.

THAT'S IT, WE'RE THROUGH

NO MORE TALK YOU

LET'S GET THE GIRL AND GO...

PETEY.

NO!

*(***PETEY*** again takes them all on a wild run through the snow. At one point he lands on* **EVE***'s shoulder. They grab both of them. She's caught! [This can be, and should be fun and unexpected])*

(Just at this point **BLACK EYED JOHNNY** *enters with* **JIMMY JACK.***)*

BLACK EYED JOHNNY. Good work men.

(He blows his whistle)

(TX: #18 ***SAIL ON MARCH****)*

(The rest of the **PIRATES** *return to the stage, each having captured an* **ELF** *or two.)*

(As all the **ELVES** *are brought together on stage,* **SANTA** *enters and the entire stage freezes with his HO HO HO.)*

SANTA CLAUS. Ho, ho, ho!

ELVES. SANTA!

SANTA CLAUS. What's going on here?

BLACK EYED JOHNNY. What do you mean Ho, ho, ho? It's Yo, ho, ho.

SANTA CLAUS. I beg to differ with you, young man. It's Ho, ho, ho.

BLACK EYED JOHNNY. *(to* **TUSK***)* Is he kiddin?

RUBY RED. Look at what he's wearin'. I'd say he's pretty serious.

SANTA CLAUS. What's the meaning of all this. Why is Mrs. Claus tied up? Do you know what day it is?

BLACK EYED JOHNNY. Is that like one of them trick questions and then next you ask me who's president?

TUSK. Don't ask him who's president. That always makes him angry.

JUNKMAN JAKE. Boo way! Ah ken day bag boobley rid efflie mate. (*But wait! I know that big bubbly red elf guy.*)

WINKY. Yeah, I think I've seen him somewhere before.

TUSK. (*to* **SANTA**) You ever been on a "Most Wanted" poster?

SANTA CLAUS. No.

JIMMY JACK. You ever appear on "Dancing With the Stars"?

MRS. SANTA. (*laughing*) No.

(**GRAINNE** *has made her way up to beside* **SANTA**. *She looks him over.*)

GRAINNE O'MALLY. You ever spend much time in the malls?

SANTA CLAUS. Why yes. Lots.

WINKY. But that's not it. It was somethin' about a chimney.

SANTA CLAUS. Perhaps this will clear things up. HO, HO HO! Does that help?

(*Music: TX: #19* ***YO HO HO / HO HO HO***)

BLACK EYED JOHNNY. Blisterin' Barnicles, I've told ya' once and I won't tell ye' again. It's YO HO HO!

PIRATES. (*sings*)
YO, HO HO, AND A BOTTLE OF RUM
IT'S A PIRATES' SONG
A FEE FIE FOE FUM
TO MARCH YE OFF THE PLANK TO THE FIFE AND DRUM
TO THE HUNGRY SHARKS YOU'LL COME

YO, HO HO, AND A FIDDLE DE DEE
IT'S A PIRATES' WAY
THE SCOURGE OF THE SEA
TO PILLAGE AND TO LOOT FILLS OUR HEARTS WITH GLEE
AND PIRATES WE'LL ALWAYS BE

ELVES.

> HO, HO HO FULL OF CHRISTMAS CHEER
> SANTA'S SONG WE ALL LOVE TO HEAR
> THE SOUND OF SHARING, OF JOYFUL PREPARING
> FOR SANTA'S MAGICAL SLEIGH TO APPEAR
>
> HO, HO HO FULL OF CHRISTMAS JOYS
> FOR THE GOOD LITTLE GIRLS AND BOYS
> THE SOUND OF SINGING, OF SLEIGH BELLS RINGING
> FOR SANTA'S BRINGING HIS BAG FULL OF TOYS

PIRATES.

> YO, HO HO AND A FIDDLE DE DUM

ELVES.

> HO, HO HO CHRISTMAS TIME HAS COME

PIRATES.

> IT'S A PIRATE'S DUTY TO STEAL ALL YOUR BOOTY

ELVES.

> JUST WAIT YOUR TURN AND WE'LL GLADLY GIVE YOU SOME

PIRATES.

> YO, HO HO BLAST YOUR COLD AND YOUR ICE

ELVES.

> HO, HO HO SANTA'S PARADISE

PIRATES.

> WE'LL PILFER AND WE'LL PLUNDER
> WE'LL TEAR THIS PLACE ASUNDER

TUSK. What the devil does that mean?

BLACK EYED JOHNNY. I don't know. It just sounded good.

ELVES.

> HE'S CHECKING HIS LIST TO SEE WHO'S NAUGHTY AND
>   NICE

PIRATES.

> YO, HO HO

ELVES.

> HO, HO HO

> *(The two groups sing against each other: YO HO HO
> vs. HO HO HO until the song erupts into a counter-
> point of each group singing their theme verse.)*

(By the end, the **ELVES** *have tied up the* **PIRATES**, *who are in a group on the floor. [They were so busy performing that didn't notice the fact that they've been tied up.])*

BLACK EYED JOHNNY. Ye cutthroat catfish, what have ye done?

TUSK. They've tied us up.

BLACK EYED JOHNNY. I can see that.

RUBY RED. What're we gonna do, Black Eyed Johnny?

SANTA CLAUS. I'll tell you what you're going to do. You're going to stay there all tied up until you learn how to be nice.

BLACK EYED JOHNNY. Nice? Now why would a pirate want to be gettin' nice?

SANTA CLAUS. Because being nice is nicer than not being nice.

TUSK. But if you're not being nice then what are you being?

HAPPY. Naughty!

BLACK EYED JOHNNY. And what's wrong with being naughty? We're pirates, that's what we do. Right men?

PIRATES. RIGHT!

BLACK EYED JOHNNY. We're naughty!

PIRATES. NAUGHTY!

MURRAY. Then you won't get any Christmas presents from Santa.

BLACK EYED JOHNNY. Well, he's not exactly giving them out anyway, now is he?

EVE. He will tonight. It's Christmas eve.

BLACK EYED JOHNNY. What's Christmas eve?

MURRAY. What's Christmas Eve? Where did you grow up, under a rock?

TUSK. Oooh, touchy subject.

BLACK EYED JOHNNY. As a matter of fact, yes.

WINKY. That's why we call him snake.

RUBY RED. That's not why we call him snake.

JIMMY JACK. Then why DO we call him snake?

(*The* **PIRATES** *all begin arguing why they call* **JOHNNY** *"Snake."* **MRS. SANTA** *interrupts them.*)

MRS. SANTA. Excuse me! Have you never had a Christmas tree?

THE PIRATES. No.

MRS. SANTA. Have you never gotten a Christmas present?

THE PIRATES. No.

MRS. SANTA. Have you never seen reindeer fly?

BLACK EYED JOHNNY. (*to* **SANTA**) Is she okay?

MURRAY. Santa, we don't have a lot of time. What're we gonna do with them? We have to get back to packing the sled. It's almost time for the reindeer to be hitched up.

(**HOLLY,** *who has slipped away during the previous scene, comes running onto the stage.*)

HOLLY. Santa! Santa!

SANTA CLAUS. What is it Holly?

(*She whispers into his ear.* **SANTA** *looks away and then to the* **PIRATES**.)

BLACK EYED JOHNNY. What? What is it ye lunatic land lubber?

(**SANTA** *pulls the others aside and talks to them.*)

SANTA CLAUS. We have an even bigger problem than the pirates.

MURRAY. What's that Santa?

SANTA CLAUS. (*looking at* **MURRAY**) Aren't you the elf in charge of the reindeer...um...

MURRAY. I clean up their...stables, yes? Why, what's the matter?

SANTA CLAUS. Every one of them is sick. Dasher is sneezing, Dancer is wheezing, Prancer just found out that he has vertigo, and Vixen...well...

(*He looks at* **MRS. CLAUS** *and doesn't want to say what's happening with Vixen.*)

SANTA CLAUS. Vixen is, well she's...

MRS. SANTA. What's wrong with Vixen?

SANTA CLAUS. Vixen is on strike.

HAPPY. Strike?

MURRAY. Why?

SANTA CLAUS. Because I let Rudolph go to Florida for the weekend once I knew we were going to have good weather.

MRS. SANTA. I told you not to do that.

SANTA CLAUS. I know, I know.

MRS. SANTA. You never listen to me.

HAPPY. They never do.

GRAINNE O'MALLY. Isn't that the truth.

BLACK EYED JOHNNY. Excuse me?

GRAINNE O'MALLY. You never listen to anything I tell you. You always think you know best.

MRS. SANTA. *(to* **SANTA***)* And that goes for you too. I told you that it wasn't fair to give Rudolph a day off when Vixen hasn't had a Christmas Eve off in over 300 years. You always favor the boys.

GRAINNE O'MALLY. Well, that's just not right.

(**GRAINNE** *lets herself out of the rope cluster and ties it tighter on the others.*)

MRS. SANTA. That's what I told him.

MURRAY. Well I think Santa has the right to give a night off to whoever he wants.

SANTA CLAUS. Thank you Murray.

HAPPY. Oh you do, do you?

MURRAY. Yes, I do.

EVE. But that doesn't seem fair, Daddy, not even to me.

HAPPY. It's not honey.

GRAINNE O'MALLY. That's right, it's not.

MRS. SANTA. No it's not! And let me tell you, things would be different around here if women made the decisions.

GRAINNE O'MALLY. Oh, you can say that again.

> (**BLACK EYED JOHNNY**, **TUSK** *and* **WINKY** *start to laugh.* **SANTA** *and* **MURRAY** *join in.*)

BLACK EYED JOHNNY. Well slap me on my Dungbee and wake me up, the woman's gone bonkers.

> (**RUBY RED** *and the other girl pirates start pummelling the men.*)

GRAINNE O'MALLY. You want bonkers? I'll give you bonkers!

(to the band)

Hit it!

*(Music: TX: #20 **IF WOMEN RULED THE WORLD**)*

> (**GRAINNE, MRS. SANTA, HAPPY** *and* **EVE** *begin to sing,* IF WOMEN RULED THE WORLD.)

GRAINNE O'MALLY.
> WHEN WILL YOU MEN EVER GET IT
> ALL YOUR MOTHERS MUST REGRET IT
> BREECHIN' BIRTH TO SUCH A BARNACLED BUNCH OF
>   FOOLS

HAPPY.
> TEN THOUSAND YEARS WE'VE TRIED TO FIGHT ON
> GET YOUR MINDS TO TURN THE LIGHT ON

ALL FOUR.
> AND PLAY THIS GAME BY A WHOLE NEW SET OF RULES

(The tempo changes to a swing, as the women move into "Andrew Sisters" mode.)

> IF WOMEN RULED THE WORLD
> WE WOULD ALL DRINK TEA WITH PINKIES RAISED
> YOU'D BE AMAZED AT HOW THIS WORLD COULD BE

GRAINNE O'MALLY. *(to* **HAPPY***)* Tell us sister.

MRS. SANTA.
> 'CAUSE NO BED WOULD BE LEFT UNMADE
> IF LIFE GAVE US LEMONS, WE'D MAKE LEMONADE

ALL FOUR.
> THAT'S THE WAY IT'D BE IF WOMEN RULED THE WORLD
> IF WOMEN RULED THE WORLD

EVE.

> EVERY BOY WOULD HAVE TO WAIT HIS TURN
> AND LEARN IT WASN'T NICE TO PULL YOUR HAIR

GRAINNE O'MALLY. *(to* **BLACK EYED JOHNNY***)*

> IF THEY'D LET US VOTE IN THEIR ELECTIONS
> WE'D NEVER BE LOST, CAUSE WE'D ASK DIRECTIONS

TUSK. *(to* **JOHNNY***)* She has you there.

BLACK EYED JOHNNY. You're the one who got us lost!

ALL FOUR.

> THAT'S THE WAY IT'D BE IF WOMEN RULED THE WORLD

(The other women join in on the bridge.)

WOMEN.

> NO MORE SPITTING, NO MORE CURSES

EVE.

> AND EVERYONE WOULD CARRY PURSES

WOMEN.

> SHOW THEIR FEELINGS, EVEN CRYING

HAPPY.

> TALKING WOULD REQUIRE REPLYING

MURRAY. I reply! I reply!

WOMEN.

> WE'D HAVE A QUEEN, SHE'D HAVE HER COURT
> BALLET WOULD BE THE OFFICIAL SPORT
> AND NO MORE LOCKS, OUR LAW DECREES
> SO MEN WOULD NEVER LOSE THEIR KEYS

ALL FOUR. Speaking of keys, KEY CHANGE!

(The entire female cast break into dance. **SANTA** *and* **MURRAY** *join in.)*

WOMEN.

> IF WOMEN RULED THE WORLD
> EVERY MAN WOULD WASH BEHIND HIS EARS
> AND HE'D GET TEN YEARS FOR NOT PICKING UP HIS JOCK

EVE. Eeeew!

WOMEN.

> NO DIRTY DISH LEFT IN THE SINK
> IF THE SEAT'S LEFT UP

GRAINNE O'MALLY.
> YOU'LL BE IN THE DRINK

WOMEN.
> ALL CREDIT CARDS COME WITHOUT A LIMIT
> ANY MAN WITH A BEARD WOULD HAVE TO TRIM IT

MRS. SANTA. You hear that, Claus?

WOMEN.
> THINGS NEAT AND PRIM, IF WOMEN RULED THE WORLD
> THAT'S HOW IT'D BE IF WOMEN...

EVE. And little girls!

ALL FOUR.
> RULED THE WORLD!

SANTA CLAUS. (*to* **MRS. CLAUS**) Alright then, if you're going to rule the world, what are you going to do about the Reindeer? How am I supposed to deliver the presents if I don't have a fleet of flying deer?

MURRAY. I don't understand it. They didn't seem sick this morning.

SANTA CLAUS. Well they're sick now.

HAPPY. Well, we have to deliver the toys. What would Christmas be without all the little girls and boys around the world waking up on Christmas morning and finding love underneath their trees?

EVE. Why don't we ask the pirates to help.

MURRAY. Oh sweetie, that's not a good idea.

GRAINNE O'MALLY. (*to* **MURRAY**) Why don't you take a caulk and put a cork in it? Go on, sweetie. You'll never know if you don't try.

MURRAY. Wait a minute, why are you telling her to ask them to help us? You're one of them.

GRAINNE O'MALLY. I'm not so sure who I am right now. I'm takin' a break and seein' how the mast unwrinkles.

BLACK EYED JOHNNY. Oh really? Well, doesn't that just burn your britches, mates?

> (*The* **PIRATES** *all react to* **GRAINNE**'*s possible turning on them.* **EVE** *steps in and clears her throat.*)

EVE. Excuse me. I'm sorry to bother you at a time like this. I mean I can see that you're not happy.

BLACK EYED JOHNNY. You can see that, can you?

EVE. Oh yes.

BLACK EYED JOHNNY. Alright, let's get this over with. What do you want to ask me?

EVE. Are you busy tonight?

BLACK EYED JOHNNY. Actually, it looks like we'll be tied up tonight. What did you have in mind?

EVE. If we untied you, would you promise to help Santa deliver all the toys around the world tonight in your pirate ship?

BLACK EYED JOHNNY. That's impossible. Our ship couldn't make it all the way around the world and back in one night. Are ye daft, you little elf ye?

MRS. SANTA. Actually, it could.

MURRAY. No, Mrs. Claus, I don't think this is a good idea.

(**SANTA** *looks out at the pirate ship.*)

SANTA CLAUS. You know something, it just might work.

MURRAY. But Santa, how do you know if we can trust them?

(*The* **PIRATES** *all smile.*)

SANTA CLAUS. They'd have to promise.

(*The* **PIRATES** *all start laughing.*)

PIRATES. A promise. Walk me to the edge of the plank if I break me promise. Oh, I'll promise ye anything...ye slumpy snail, ye.

(**MRS. CLAUS** *steps to the foot of the stage and sprays magic snow into the air.*)

(*TX: #21* ***CHRISTMAS IS ALL ABOUT THE LOVE***)

(*The pirate ship starts to levitate.*)

BLACK EYED JOHNNY. How did you do that? Are ye a witch?

EVE. No. She's Mrs. Santa Claus.

HOLLY & IVY. And it's Christmas Eve.

HAPPY. The most magical day of the year.

SANTA CLAUS. Every year on Christmas eve we all become filled with the power of giving, of making people smile, laugh, filling them with the joy of Christmas cheer. Love can do many things...

(*beat*)

EVE. ...even make pirate ships fly.

(*sings*)

CHRISTMAS IS ALL ABOUT THE JOYS
THE GIFTS FOR GIRLS AND BOYS
UNDERNEATH THE CHRISTMAS TREE
CHRISTMAS IS ALL ABOUT THE LOVE
THE REINDEER FLYING UP ABOVE THE SKY
CHRISTMAS IS SOMETHING IN THE AIR
THE MOMENTS THAT WE SHARE
WHEN WE TAKE EACH OTHER'S HANDS

EVE, HOLLY & IVY.

AND CHRISTMAS IS SOMETHING IN YOUR HEART
THE FEELING THAT WE'RE PART OF SOMETHING MORE

ADD MURRAY & HAPPY.

THAT'S WHAT CHRISTMAS IS REALLY FOR

ADD SANTA & MRS. SANTA.

(**PIRATES** *OOH*)

IT'S A TIME FOR EVERYONE
TO STOP AND HAVE SOME FUN
A TIME WHEN ALL THE WORLD IS AT PEACE
IT'S A TIME TO THINK OF LOVE
TO SEE THE STARS ABOVE

EVE.

AND REMEMBER WE ARE ALL A PART
OF SOMETHING WE CAN'T SEE

(*The* **PIRATES** *have all fallen apart and are now crying. They sing*)

PIRATES.

CHRISTMAS IS ALL ABOUT THE JOYS
THE GIFTS FOR GIRLS AND BOYS
UNDERNEATH THE CHRISTMAS TREE

EVERYONE.
> CHRISTMAS IS ALL ABOUT THE LOVE
> THE REINDEER FLYING UP ABOVE THE SKY
> THAT'S WHAT CHRISTMAS IS ALL ABOUT

> *(The* **PIRATES** *all begin to cry as the* **ELVES** *surround them. Little* **EVE** *crawls into* **JOHNNY***'s lap and puts her arm around him.)*

> *(***GRAINNE** *steps in between* **SANTA** *and* **MRS. CLAUS** *and hugs them both.)*

BLACK EYED JOHNNY. But I grew up under a rock. It was cold and slimy. I never knew what it was like to have love and joy in me heart.

TUSK. Every year I would wake up one morning and find coal in my socks and I never knew why. Now I know. It's because I was NAUGHTY!

RUBY RED. I was raised in an orphanage and we never got presents.

WINKY. I always wanted a BB-gun but my parents wouldn't buy me one because they said I only had one eye left and I couldn't afford the risk.

JIMMY JACK. *(hitting* **JOHNNY***)* How come you never told me about Christmas? It's the happiest day of the year and you never told me about it.

JUNKMAN JAKE. D'oly presie ah airrrrr goat wiz haggis! *(All I ever got was haggis!)*

TUSK. Petey's never had a real cracker in his whole life. He deserves a present.

EVE. Everyone deserves presents. That's what Christmas is all about.

> *(During the next section,* **EVE** *and the* **ELVES** *untie the* **PIRATES***. Everyone fills the stage with song.)*

EVERYONE.
> IT'S A TIME FOR EVERYONE
> TO STOP AND HAVE SOME FUN
> A TIME WHEN ALL THE WORLD IS AT PEACE
> IT'S A TIME TO THINK OF LOVE
> TO SEE THE STARS ABOVE

JOHNNY & EVE.
> AND REMEMBER WE ARE ALL A PART
> OF SOMETHING WE CAN'T SEE

EVERYONE.
> CHRISTMAS IS ALL ABOUT THE JOYS
> THE GIFTS FOR GIRLS AND BOYS
> UNDERNEATH THE CHRISTMAS TREE
>
> AND CHRISTMAS IS ALL ABOUT THE LOVE
> THE REINDEER FLYING UP ABOVE THE SKY
> THAT'S WHAT CHRISTMAS IS ALL ABOUT
> THAT'S WHAT CHRISTMAS IS ALL ABOUT

> *(**GRAINNE** and **JOHNNY** come together in an embrace.*
> ***JIMMY JACK** comes to them and hugs them both.)*

> *(**EVE** steps forward and speaks to **JOHNNY**.)*

EVE. Well, Mr. Black Eyed Johnny, will you help us?

GRAINNE O'MALLY. Of course he will.

BLACK EYED JOHNNY. *(blowing up and then calming down)* Blubberin' cactus, if ye intend on rulin' the world, you'll have to be sharin' it with me. Equal parts! You get the bowsprit, I get the Fo'c's'le! Deal?

GRAINNE O'MALLY. Deal!

BLACK EYED JOHNNY. *(to **EVE**)* Now go on 'n ask me again?

EVE. Will you help us?

BLACK EYED JOHNNY. As sure as my name is Black Eyed Johnny, we'll help you get them toys to all the girls and boys in the world. And we'll do it while there's still the stars in the sky and the moon to guide us.

TUSK. And Petey can lead the way, Right Petey?

PETEY. Aye, aye, captain!

RUBY RED. It wouldn't be Christmas without the presents.

JUNKMAN JAKE. Aidh! *(Yes)*

WINKY. You can count on Winky!

GRAINNE O'MALLY. *(to **WINKY**)* Don't do the third person thing, it really weird's me out.

BLACK EYED JOHNNY. You can count on all of us.

SANTA CLAUS. Promise?

PIRATES. We promise!

> (SANTA *and the* ELVES *cheer. The* PIRATES *start to pull out all of the bags of toys for the ship.*)

> (*Music: Instrumental of* **CHRISTMAS IS ALL ABOUT THE LOVE**)

> (*TX: #22* **CHRISTMAS UNDERSCORE**)

> (HAPPY *pulls* GRAINNE *aside.*)

HAPPY. (*to* GRAINNE) Thank you so much for making this happen.

GRAINNE O'MALLY. Twas nothin'! I been lookin' to careen this motley crew for quite some time now. All we needed was a little direction, that's all.

> (*She makes a motion of turning around the map.*)

HAPPY. You mean...

GRAINNE O'MALLY. Aye. I turned the map around while Tusk wasn't lookin', which is most of the time. I heard there was a special kind of magic on this island. What I heard was true. There is.

HAPPY. Oh, Granny.

GRAINNE O'MALLY. Grainne! It's not Granny, it's Grainne. There's no Y...it's just...oh what the heck. Granny's fine!

> (GRAINNE *and* HAPPY *hug.*)

> (SANTA *makes a grand entrance dressed for the all-night delivery. Everyone cheers. He addresses the* PIRATES, *who have assembled in formation in front of the* ELVES.)

SANTA CLAUS. Thank you Black Eyed Johnny. With your help and the help of your family, we will be able to spread love and spirit throughout all the world this night. It will be a Merry Christmas that begins on this Happy Christmas Eve.

BLACK EYED JOHNNY. Don't thank me. Thank her.

> (*pointing to* EVE)

You really know how to sing a song, Eve.

(beat)

Wait a minute! Shiver me timbers, I just got it.

(pointing to each person as he speaks)

Murray Christmas, Happy Christmas, the Holly and the Ivy, Eve Christmas...

WINKY. Wait a minute. That one doesn't work. Eve Christmas, it's backwards.

BLACK EYED JOHNNY. No, it's like the phone book, the last name comes first. Eve Christmas - Christmas Eve, see?

WINKY. Oh, now I get it!

BLACK EYED JOHNNY. You ARE Christmas Eve...all of you. Each and every one of you.

SANTA CLAUS. No! Each and every one of US. It's one for all and all for one now, eh? Yo Ho Ho and all that stuff?

BLACK EYED JOHNNY. If you say so. Alright ye pirate elves. Let's raise the yardarm and sail 'er into the sunrise!

*(TX: #23 **SAIL ON FINALE**)*

*(**BLACK EYED JOHNNY** and **EVE** step into a pool of light and sing. The others climb on board the Flyin' Dutchperson.)*

BLACK EYED JOHNNY & EVE.
IF SAILOR TALES AND SAILOR TUNES
IF PIRATES, SCHOONERS AND DUBLOONS
BUCCANEERS AND BURIED GOLD
BLOOD AND SWASH AND STORIES TOLD
IF YOU'VE A THIRST FOR GORE AND GRIME
THEN I'VE A TALE TO PASS THE TIME
SO GATHER ROUND, DON'T BREATHE A WORD
A STORY YOU HAVE NEVER HEARD
COME BOARD OUR SHIP WE'LL SAIL AWAY

*(The **PIRATES** and **SANTA** put their rubber tubes on and climb out into the water to board the ship, all carrying bags of toys.)*

*(**SANTA** throws goodies to all the children as they make their way up the aisles and into the sky.)*

COMPANY. *(they sing)*
SAIL ON, SAIL ON
TO MAKE THE CHILDREN SMILE
SAIL ON, SAIL ON
FROM THE LAND OF CHRISTMAS ISLE
(Everyone makes their way off stage, as **EVE** *gets back into bed. The music fades into sleigh bells...)*
(By this point the lights are fading and we are back at the top of the pay with **EVE** *in her bed)*
*(***EVE*** wakes up startled from her dream.)*
(She crosses to her window and looks out, watching for **SANTA** *in the sky.)*

EVE. Good luck, Black Eyed Johnny. See you when you get to my house. Yo Ho Ho!

*(The music segues into **CHRISTMAS IS ALL ABOUT THE LOVE**)*

*(***HAPPY*** *and* **MURRAY** *enter the room.)*

HAPPY. Eve! What are you doing?

MURRAY. She's looking for reindeer, I'll bet.

EVE. Actually, I'm looking for the pirates. They're helping Santa deliver the presents this year.

MURRAY. Pirates are delivering the presents?

EVE. Yes, a whole bunch of them. And some of them were GIRL PIRATES.

HAPPY. Girl pirates, huh?

MURRAY. Sure. That makes sense.

EVE. It does?

MURRAY. Absolutely. In fact... *(beat)* ...I think I heard something on the front porch. Perhaps...

*(***MURRAY*** *runs out of the room.)*

HAPPY. Murray, where are you going?

*(***EVE*** *starts to follow* **MURRAY** *out of the room.* **HAPPY** *takes her into her arms.)*

HAPPY. *(to* **EVE***)* No, no young lady. You have to get back
into bed.

   (calling after **MURRAY***)*

   Murray?

EVE. Mom, you should have been there. There was a pirate
ship and a whirlpool. And they were trying to steal
Santa's toys. But then Grainne turned the map around.

HAPPY. Granny? She was there?

EVE. NO! Not Granny...Grainne. There's a big difference.
And you and Dad were elves and Dad was in charge of
the reindeers...well, sort of.

HAPPY. He was?

EVE. And Tusk had a singing parrot. And Winky could tap
dance...

HAPPY. Tap dancing pirates?

EVE. Yes, and Aunt Mary was Mrs. Claus and Uncle Al was
Santa...

   *(***HOLLY** *and* **IVY** *enter, sleepy eyed)*

IVY. Why is everyone awake?

HOLLY. What time is it?

EVE. And you guys were there too and you were sort of
exactly the way you are.

   *(***MURRAY** *re-enters with a giant pirate ship filled with
   pirates.)*

EVE. OH MY GOODNESS! MY PIRATE SHIP!

   *(***EVE** *screams as* **MURRAY** *puts the pirate ship on the bed
   and starts to play with* **EVE.***)*

   Where did you find it?

MURRAY. It was on the front porch. Santa must have left it
for you.

EVE. No. It was Black Eyed Johnny.

   *(***HAPPY** *looks on smiling.* **EVE** *steps off the bed and over
   to the window. She looks out and catches a glimpse of
   something.)*

(From above it all, **BLACK EYED JOHNNY** *steps into a pool of light. He and* **EVE** *catch one another's eyes. They both sing.)*

BLACK EYED JOHNNY.

THAT'S WHAT CHRISTMAS IS ALL ABOUT.

BLACK EYED JOHNNY & EVE.

THAT'S WHAT CHRISTMAS IS ALL ABOUT.

BLACK EYED JOHNNY.

YO HO HO! MERRY CHRISTMAS!

EVE.

ARGGH!

THE END

(TX: #24 **CURTAIN CALL***)*

YO HO HO - TRACKS LIST

CUE TITLES	RUNNING TIME
1. Show Opening	0:39
2. *I WOULDN'T MIND*	3:22
3. Johnny's Entrance	1:08
4. *SAIL ON*	4:58
5. Whirlpool FX	1:05
6. Cold Wind	5:01
7. *SNOW*	3:57
8. The Shield #1	0:04
9. Sail On Playoff - Eve's Entrance	0:43
10. Ship Disappears	0:10
11. *WHERE ARE THEY NOW?*	2:36
12. Where Are They Now? Playoff	0:18
13. The Shield #2	0:04
14. Mrs. Claus #1	0:17
15. Mrs. Claus #2	0:17
16. The Chase	1:51
17. *PETEY'S SONG*	2:47
18. Sail On March	0:40
19. *YO HO HO / HO HO HO*	2:55
20. *IF WOMEN RULED THE WORLD*	3:10
21. *CHRISTMAS IS ALL ABOUT THE LOVE*	5:04
22. Christmas Underscore	3:38
23. *SAIL ON FINALE*	3:14
24. Curtain Call	2:27